SOJOURNER TRUTH

Other titles in the
PEOPLE WHO MADE A DIFFERENCE
series include

Louis Braille
Marie Curie
Father Damien
Mahatma Gandhi
Bob Geldof
Martin Luther King, Jr.
Ralph Nader
Florence Nightingale
Albert Schweitzer
Mother Teresa
Desmond Tutu

A Gareth Stevens Children's Books edition

Edited, designed, and produced by
Gareth Stevens Children's Books
1555 North RiverCenter Drive, Suite 201
Milwaukee, Wisconsin 53212, USA

First published in the United States and Canada in 1991 by
Gareth Stevens, Inc. This edition is abridged from *Sojourner
Truth: The courageous former slave whose eloquence helped
promote human equality*, published in 1990 by Gareth Stevens,
Inc., and written by Susan Taylor-Boyd. Text, end matter,
and format copyright © 1990 by Gareth Stevens, Inc.

For a free color catalog describing
Gareth Stevens' list of high-quality
children's books, call

1-800-341-3569 (USA) or
1-800-461-9120 (Canada)

PICTURE CREDITS
The Bettmann Archive — 18, 31; Sharon
Burris © Gareth Stevens, Inc., 1989 — 20;
Historical Pictures Service, Chicago —
10, 26, 35, 42, 59; Library of Congress —
14, 16, 22, 43 (both); Courtesy of the
Louisiana State Museum — 6; Bernice B.
Lowe Collection, Michigan Historical
Collections, Bentley Historical Library,
University of Michigan — 4, 13
(bottom), 27, 28, 32, 33, 38, 51;
Milwaukee County Historical Society —
9, 13 (top), 29, 30, 37; Missouri Historical
Society — 25, 45; Courtesy of the New
York Historical Society, New York City
— 24 (top and bottom), 41, 49; Tom
Redman — cover illustration;
Schomburg Center for Research in Black
Culture, The New York Public Library,
Astor, Lenox and Tilden Foundations —
11; UPI/Bettmann Newsphotos — 53,
55, 56, 57.

The reproduction rights to all
photographs and illustrations in
this book are controlled by the
individuals or institutions credited
above and may not be reproduced
without their permission.

Library of Congress Cataloging-in-Publication Data

Tolan, Mary M., 1952-
    Sojourner Truth / Mary M. Tolan's adaptation of the book by
Susan Taylor-Boyd. — North American ed.
        p. cm. — (People who made a difference)
    Includes bibliographical references and index.
    Summary: Follows the life of the former slave who gained
renown as an abolitionist and advocate of women's rights.
    ISBN 0-8368-0458-9
    1. Truth, Sojourner, d. 1883—Juvenile literature. 2. Afro-
Americans—Biography—Juvenile literature. 3. Abolitionists—
United States—Biography—Juvenile literature. 4. Social
reformers—United States—Biography—Juvenile literature. [1.
Truth, Sojourner, d. 1883. 2. Abolitionists. 3. Reformers. 4. Afro-
Americans—Biography.] I. Taylor-Boyd, Susan, 1949- . Sojourner
Truth. II. Title. III. Series.
E185.97.T8T65   1990   305.5'67'092—dc20
[B]   [92]   90-37922

Series conceived by Helen Exley
Series editor: Amy Bauman
Editorial assistants: Scott Enk, Diane Laska, John D. Rateliff
Cover design: Kate Kriege
Layout: Kristi Ludwig
Picture research: Daniel Helminak

Printed in the United States of America

1 2 3 4 5 6 7 8 9 9 94 93 92 91

SOJOURNER TRUTH

The courageous former slave who led others to freedom

Mary
Tolan

Susan
Taylor-Boyd

Gareth Stevens Children's Books
MILWAUKEE

Raising her voice

"I want to ride! I want to ride!" yelled the elderly black woman. The white people riding the Washington, D.C., streetcar watched her run after the car. She was shaking her cane and shouting at the white driver. It was 1867. The Civil War was over, and the American slaves had been freed by law.

But laws don't always change people's feelings. Many conductors, as well as other people, were still prejudiced against African-Americans. This means they hated black people because of the color of their skin. So even though streetcars were supposed to be for everyone, conductors often refused to stop for African-Americans. But this black woman named Sojourner Truth wasn't about to let anybody refuse her anything just because she was black. She ran after the streetcar and jumped onto it.

"Get out of the way and let this lady through," the conductor yelled once she was on the streetcar. But he was talking about a white woman behind Truth.

"I'm a lady, too!" Truth shouted back and took a seat.

Sojourner spent her life fighting battles like this. No difficulty was too big for her

"She was fearless in the face of danger, biting in her wit, sharp in her attacks, pointed in her arguments; tender when necessary but never weak."
Victoria Ortiz,
in Sojourner Truth,
A Self-Made Woman

Opposite: This engraving of Sojourner Truth as a young woman was created from the artist's imagination. As a slave, Truth would not have been wealthy enough to have such an engraving done.

to overcome — especially when it involved human rights. During her lifetime, she had seen laws passed to free black people and protect their basic human rights. But she knew even more changes were needed, and she was not afraid to fight for them. "I go for agitating," she once said.

The work begun by Sojourner Truth continues even today. Many groups, inspired by her, still fight for basic rights for all people. Sojourner Truth would be amazed and pleased to see the far-reaching effects of her work.

"Slaves, horses, and other cattle"

Sojourner Truth was born a slave in 1797 in Ulster County, New York. Her parents, Elizabeth (called Mau-Mau Bett)

This painting shows a Southern plantation that was much bigger than the Northern farms where Truth lived and worked. Fewer slaves were needed on small farms than on large plantations. Farm slaves usually lived in the owner's basement. Plantation slaves usually lived in shacks, separate from the main house.

and James (known as Baumfree) named her Isabella, but everyone called her Belle. She was their eleventh child.

Belle and her family belonged to Colonel Charles Hardenbergh. Life was hard. They worked long hours but never had enough food or clothing. Their home was a damp, dirty basement that they shared with all the other slaves. It was cold in the winter and too hot in the summer. And there was always fear. Slaves lived in fear of being beaten by their masters, or worse yet, being sold.

To help her children get through hard times, Mau-Mau Bett taught them to pray. She told them, "When you are beaten, or cruelly treated, or fall into any trouble, you must ask help of God, and he will always hear and help you." Mau-Mau Bett had strong faith in God.

At first Belle wasn't so sure about God. But then she began to talk to him every day. When she was confused or in pain, she would ask God to help her. Later, she would say, "My good Master kept me for he had something for me to do."

One of Belle's first hardships was when the Hardenberghs sold her. Belle was the Hardenberghs' kitchen slave. Sometimes she didn't do exactly as she was told. So when she was nine they took her to an auction. That is an event where people can buy and sell all kinds of goods. "Slaves, horses, and other

"The purchase of a Negro was usually to secure a wife [for] one of his men or to get a specially skilled blacksmith or carpenter. It was always to add to the ... efficiency of the plantation rather than to acquire a large number of slaves."
Nellie Thomas McColl, remembering her grandfather's plantation

7

cattle will be sold," read the auction sign. A man named John Neely bought her. This was the first of many times that Belle would be sold.

No more parents

Belle felt terribly sad about leaving her parents. Even though Neely's farm was close to the Hardenberghs', she knew she might never see her family again. Slave owners did not often allow slaves to visit one another. Slaves were expected to work hard all the time. Belle saw her parents only three more times in her life.

When the Hardenberghs sold Belle, they freed her parents. But Mau-Mau Bett and Baumfree could not just walk away and start a new life. They did not know how. They were used to living in that dark, damp basement with other slaves. So they just stayed there.

Belle was also having a hard time. The Neelys spoke English. But Belle spoke only Dutch because the Hardenberghs were Dutch. So Belle did not understand what her new master said to her. Neely thought she was acting stupid on purpose. So he beat her.

Belle never forgot those beatings. Later, when she was grown, she talked about them. She talked to people who were fighting for women's rights. "Oh, my God, what a way is this of treating human beings?" she would ask.

Soon Neely sold Belle, and then her new owner sold her again. This time, a man named John Dumont bought her. She was just thirteen years old.

Black potatoes

Belle's years as the Dumonts' slave were important to her. Something happened to her on their farm that she never forgot. She later said it proved that God watched over innocent people.

At the Dumonts', Belle was a kitchen slave. Mrs. Dumont's white servant, Kate, also worked in the kitchen. She was jealous because Belle did such a good job. So Kate decided to get Belle in trouble. One of Belle's jobs was to boil potatoes for the Dumont family each day. And each day, the potatoes came out black. No matter how careful Belle was, the potatoes would always be ruined.

Then one day the Dumonts' daughter, Gertrude, caught Kate throwing ashes into the potato pot. Gertrude ran to tell her father, and Kate was punished.

Gertrude's kindness made Belle happy. For the first time in Belle's life, a white person had treated her fairly. She believed God was watching out for her.

True love and a forced marriage

Another important yet sad event in Belle's life involved a slave named Robert. Robert belonged to a man named

Black families were torn apart by both slavery and the war to end it. Many whites considered blacks savages who had no family love. The owners believed that any grief the slaves felt would be quickly forgotten.

Some slave owners thought slaves were livestock. They beat and punished the slaves as if they were stubborn animals. These owners believed that "feeling the lash" would make the slaves obey.

Catlin, who owned a nearby farm. Robert and Belle fell in love.

One day, Belle became ill, and Robert visited her. He knew he wasn't allowed to, but he took the chance. When Catlin found out about the visit, he and his son caught Robert and beat him. John Dumont ordered them off his property. "I'll have no niggers* killed here," he shouted at Catlin. So they dragged Robert away. Soon after, Catlin forced Robert to marry another slave woman. Belle never saw him again.

Meanwhile, Dumont chose an old slave named Thomas for Belle to marry. Thomas had been married twice before. But Dumont had sold both of his other wives. Thomas and Belle had five children: Diana, Elizabeth, Peter, Sophie, and a fourth daughter who died as a baby. Peter was sold when he was five.

Mau-Mau Bett and Baumfree die
Belle's parents never saw their grandchildren. Mau-Mau Bett died before they were born. An infection in her leg had given her a fever. The dampness in the

---

*Niggers was a word meaning "blacks" or "African-Americans." People at the time, even Sojourner Truth, used it often. But today calling someone a "nigger" is an insult. The author and editor use it to be true to history. Please see the glossary at the end of this book for more about this and other words.

basement made it worse. One day, Baumfree found Mau-Mau Bett face down in the cellar. She had fallen and was too weak to get up. Baumfree helped her to bed, where she died. After Mau-Mau Bett died, the Hardenberghs decided Baumfree was too old and blind to work any longer. So they sent him to live in a cabin in the woods.

When Belle had her first child, she wanted to show the baby to Baumfree. One day, she walked to Hardenbergh's farm. At the farm, the family told her that Baumfree now lived in a cabin even farther away. Belle was too tired to go on. So she went back to the Dumonts'.

She never saw her father again. He was too weak to care for himself, and he starved. He died that winter. Later on, Belle told people that she learned from her father's last years that being free can be very painful.

11

Abolishing slavery

In the Northern states, some people had been fighting slavery since the early 1800s. These people worked to end, or abolish, slavery. They were called abolitionists. Machines could now do most work done on farms. People no longer needed as many slaves. But cities needed workers for factory jobs. Many people felt that the slaves should be freed and allowed to work in the factories.

Other people were very religious. They believed that it was against God's will to keep slaves. They said all people were equal in God's eyes. Belle agreed. She was also very religious. At first, she had told herself that God must have had a good reason to let slavery continue. But then she started to think that slavery was bad. She had seen so many slaves beaten and mistreated.

So she began to fight against slavery. In speeches later, she would ask, "Who made your skin white? Was it not God? Who made mine black? Was it not the same God?"

The abolitionists worked hard against slavery. In 1818, their work led to a new law in New York. This law promised freedom to all slaves in New York as of July 4, 1827. Belle danced with joy.

Then Dumont promised to free her one year early for all her hard work. In 1826, she worked even harder. She was excited about her freedom. But on July 4, 1826, Dumont changed his mind.

Running away — to freedom

Belle couldn't believe it. Dumont had broken his promise. But it did not matter. She could not bear being a slave even one more year.

Belle decided to leave Dumont's house. She was going to find work as a free woman. She would take only her baby, Sophia, with her. The older children would stay with their father. Before sunrise the next day, Belle began her journey to freedom. That journey lasted her whole life.

Belle soon found help through Isaac and Maria Van Wagener. They belonged to a religious group called Quakers. The Van Wageners, like many Quakers, were against slavery. They gladly took both Belle and her baby into their home.

Above: Quakers did not believe in slavery. Some people attacked them because of this belief.

Below: Truth could not write. She asked friends to help her keep records of her experiences.

Dumont caught up with Belle there. He accused her of running away.

"No, I took the freedom you promised me," she answered.

Dumont demanded that Belle return with him. She refused. Finally, Van Wagener paid Dumont twenty-five dollars to leave Belle and the baby alone. Belle fell at Van Wagener's feet, saying, "Thank you, master!"

"Don't call me that," he told her. "You have no master but God."

Belle was free at last.

Cotton was a valuable crop on Southern plantations. Plantation owners needed a huge work force to plant, tend, and pick the crop. Slaves were far more important to Southern plantation owners than to Northern farmers.

"I'll have my son back!"

One day, Belle learned that Dumont had sold her son, Peter. In fact, he had been

sold twice. He now belonged to Dumont's neighbor, Solomon Gedney. Belle was not worried because by the New York law of 1818, Gedney would be forced to free her son in 1827. And since it was against the law to sell a slave to a different state, Peter would be safe.

But then Belle heard that Gedney had disobeyed the law. He had sold Peter to his brother-in-law, who was a farmer in Alabama. Now Belle was upset. Peter would never be free in the South.

At once, she went to the Dumonts. She asked them to buy Peter back.

"What a fuss you make about a little nigger!" Mrs. Dumont laughed at her.

Belle was furious. "I'll have my son back!" she said.

"How?" asked Mrs. Dumont. "You have no money — nothing."

"God will help me," Belle answered.

Belle took the problem to court in Kingston, New York. There she hired a lawyer to help her. She became one of the first black people to fight a white person in an American court.

Instead of going to court, Solomon Gedney brought Peter back to New York. But he said Peter still belonged to him. So Belle took him to court again.

Belle's day in court

Belle was nervous about going to court. She knew that being both black and a

Several religious communities sprang up in the North during the early 1800s. They were built around the idea of equality. Members shared property and all worked in a common industry. The most famous of these colonies was Oneida, New York. This colony produced silverware. The colony broke up, but the industry remains today.

woman worked against her. She knew that blacks and women often did not receive equal justice. But she had no other choice. She would trust in God and the judge.

Peter was scared, too. In the courtroom, he would not go to Belle. He clutched Gedney's legs and cried out, "She is not my mother. I want to stay with my master."

Belle was afraid she had lost her son forever. But the judge was not so sure. He could see the boy had been beaten.

"How did you get that scar on your forehead, son?" the judge asked.

"A horse kicked me," Peter answered.

"And the other scars?"

The judge guessed that Gedney had forced the boy to lie. He ordered that Peter be returned to his mother. Belle had won her son back! But she knew the fight wasn't over. She knew she would always be fighting for her rights.

The Kingdom

Now Belle had to care for Peter as well as Sophia. It was hard for a black woman to find work. Slaves filled most jobs. Other jobs did not pay enough. So in 1829, Belle took Peter and moved to New York City. Sadly, she left Sophia with Diana and Elizabeth at the Dumonts'. In the city, Belle would not be able to hold a job and care for a small child.

In the city, she found work with Elijah Pierson, a rich widower. Pierson was a religious man. He believed that God would make a kingdom of love and peace on earth. He told Belle about a prophet with long hair and a beard.

One day a long-haired, bearded man named Robert Matthews came to the door. He told Belle that God had sent him to set up a kingdom of heaven on earth. Belle and Pierson helped Matthews set up a small religious community in Sing Sing, New York. It was called the Kingdom.

But Matthews was not the prophet they expected. He was lazy and not very religious. The Kingdom was soon

In the 1840s, New York City grew rapidly. Merchants, builders, doctors, and lawyers got rich. Many of the people who had come from Europe lived in slums. But blacks who worked as servants earned enough money to stay out of them. Some groups tried to help the poor by opening shelters and food banks. But most people just didn't think about the problems.

failing. Its followers began to fight with one another. Belle realized that love and peace were goals. People had to work hard to win them.

Belle also learned that people said she was equal but did not always treat her that way. She was the only black person in the Kingdom. She also did most of the work. It was like being a slave again. And after Pierson died, Belle was shocked when her white friends turned against her. Two of them, Benjamin and Ann Folger, said that Belle had poisoned Pierson. They said she was trying to poison them, too.

Belle knew she had to defend herself against these lies. So she hired another lawyer and sued the Folgers for trying to ruin her good name with lies.

Again Belle won. The court ordered the Folgers to pay her $125 for what they had done. Once again she had fought for her rights. And once again, by trusting in God and the court, she got justice.

The ugly city

Belle left the Kingdom and returned to New York City in 1834. There, Peter began getting into trouble with the law. Belle knew that Peter's life in Alabama and with Gedney had left marks on more than his body. Inside, he was angry and confused. Things got worse every day.

"How can you expect to do good to God unless you first learn to do good to each other?"
Sojourner Truth

Finally, he was arrested and thrown in prison. He was set free when a friend found him a job on a whaling ship. Now both Belle and Peter were happy. He wrote to his mother and said that for the first time he felt truly free.

After two years, his letters stopped coming. Later, Belle learned that Peter was dead. She was miserable. She had struggled so long and hard to have him with her. After it all, he was gone forever.

Belle felt empty. Over the past few years, she had been let down by her religion, her friends, and even her son. She blamed all of this on the city. And she decided it was time to leave New York City. She wanted to go where she could get back in touch with God.

A new name, a new life

Belle felt that God was urging her to leave the city and go east. She told her employers, "The Spirit calls me there, and I must go."

By 1843, she was ready for a new life. She was forty-six years old, and her children were grown. All she had to do was care for herself — and serve God.

Belle wanted to leave her old life behind her. She even wanted a new name. "The Lord gave me Sojourner," she later said, "because I was to travel up and down the land, showing people their sins, and being a sign unto them."

Truth traveled most of the northern United States. This covered an area of thousands of square miles. Often, she traveled on foot. And often she did not know where she would be able to stop and rest.

She changed her last name, too. She knew that God was called Truth in the Bible. So she named herself Sojourner Truth. And with her new name, she began her new life.

Sojourner speaks her truth

By the time Truth began her travels that year, her family was far behind. Her husband and her son were dead. Her daughters still worked as servants on Dumont's farm.

When Truth left New York, her daughters were afraid they would not see her again. But Truth kept in touch with them. She had worked so hard to keep her family safe and free until now. She would not let her travels keep her from them.

Truth went east, taking different jobs along the way. Everywhere she went, she talked to people about God. She offered her message to anyone who would listen. But she never stayed in one place long.

Soon her preaching made her famous. By the winter of 1843, she had made it to Massachusetts. Many groups there wanted to hear her speak. One group was the Northampton Association of Education and Industry. This group's goal was to create a perfect world.

Part of that goal included doing away with slavery. Truth had never seen such a huge group of people fighting against

"Let her tell her story without interrupting her, and . . . you will see . . . that God helps her to pry where but few can. She cannot read or write, but the law is in her heart."
A church member in Bristol, Connecticut, writing to a Hartford church

22

slavery. She suddenly understood that the fight for freedom was not just her fight. It was everyone's fight.

Fighting together

When Truth first met the abolitionists in the 1820s, she was still a slave. They had encouraged her to fight for her freedom. She had. Now she wanted to do more. She wanted to help free other slaves.

At Northampton in 1843-1844, she began to hear stories of other slaves from some of the great abolitionist speakers. Among these speakers were William Lloyd Garrison and Frederick Douglass. From them and others, she heard that slaves in the South were also often beaten, and their families were being torn apart, too.

It seemed to Truth that people deserved more respect than this. Experiences from her own life had taught her this. She recalled the day that Peter came back from the Gedneys' farm covered with scars. Truth had been shocked at how little Gedney valued his slaves' lives. She also remembered how she had once prayed for revenge. When Gedney had sold Peter, Truth had prayed to God to get even with the Gedney family. After her prayer, Gedney's sister was beaten to death by her husband.

From these experiences, Truth learned to value human life. She believed that

Opposite: Some Northern black men became powerful leaders against slavery. Many women, such as Sojourner Truth, were also well-known leaders, but advertising rarely listed their work.

23

every life deserved respect. That meant that society had to treat all people as valuable. At Northampton, she decided to put some of these ideas into her preaching. After that, instead of just preaching about religion, Truth began talking about respect, freedom, and equality for everyone.

The power of her truth

But often while at Northampton, Truth just listened to the speakers. She did not get up and preach. Then one night a group of young men burst into a meeting. Like many people, they did not like the abolitionists. Truth was the only black person at the meeting. She was afraid they would beat her. So she hid.

Frightened, she began to pray. Then suddenly she thought, "Shall I run away and hide from the Devil? Me, a servant of the living God? Have I not faith enough to go out and quell the mob?"

So she walked out of the tent and to the top of a nearby hill. There she began to sing. The mob heard her strong voice and ran out after her. But as they got close to her, she shouted, "Why do you come about me with clubs and sticks? I am not doing any harm to anyone."

The people were surprised at how calm she was. So they stopped to listen. She spoke to them and answered their questions about slavery and God and the

Top: William Lloyd Garrison was an outspoken abolitionist. He used his newspaper, the Liberator, *to fight against slavery.*

Above: Frederick Douglass was an escaped slave. He described himself as "a recent graduate from the institution of slavery with his diploma on his back."

24

abolitionists. Finally, she asked them to leave in peace. Surprisingly, they did.

Sojourner Truth was no longer a frightened slave. That night she proved to everyone — especially to herself — that no one but God would ever be her master. And that night, too, she saw clearly her new job. It was to fight for freedom and equality for all people.

"Rachel had the power to move and bear down a whole audience by a few simple words. I never knew but one other human being that had that power, and that other was Sojourner Truth."

Wendell Phillips, abolitionist and social reformer

New laws

Several years after Truth left the city of Northampton, Congress passed the Fugitive Slave Law of 1850. This law said escaped slaves had no right to a trial by a jury and could not testify in court. It also made it a crime for anyone to help slaves escape. Even slaves who had escaped years before could still be arrested.

Abolitionists were furious. This law was more strict than the Fugitive Slave Act of 1793. That law said that when runaway slaves were captured, they would be returned to their owners. Between the two laws, slaves did not have much chance of being free.

In the late 1850s, a slave put these laws to the test. Dred Scott, a Southern slave, had traveled with his master to a free state. Slavery was not allowed there. After he had returned to the South, his master died. Scott sued his master's widow for his freedom. He said he should be free because he had lived in a

A photograph of Dred Scott. The Supreme Court decided against Dred Scott when he sued for his freedom. The court voted that moving from a slave state to a free state did not make a slave free.

Harriet Tubman was a member of the Underground Railroad. She led over three hundred slaves to freedom. She also worked as a spy for the Union army.

free state. The case went all the way to the United States Supreme Court.

But Scott was unlucky. The court ruled that "any Negro whose ancestors were sold as slaves" did not have the rights of a U.S. citizen. No blacks could claim their freedom.

These hurdles for African-Americans seemed too high to jump over. But the abolitionists would not give up. They formed a secret system to help slaves escape to Canada. In Canada, the U.S. laws could not affect the slaves. Through this system, slaves were moved from one hiding place, or safe house, to another on their way out of the country. This system was called the Underground Railroad.

The power of words

The abolitionists also continued their battle against slavery by speaking out. Sojourner Truth was one of their most powerful speakers.

In the years before the Civil War, Truth spoke to many audiences. In ten years, she traveled to twenty-one states and Washington, D.C. Her travels covered thousands of miles. Most of the time she had to walk, because blacks were not allowed on public coaches or trains.

Many people were not happy to hear her words. Even many of the white people who were against slavery did not want to be taught by a black person. But

This photo shows Truth's traditional gray dress, white shawl, and turban that she wore on her journeys. Many people asked if she was a woman or a man. She decided that these people would want to have a photograph to study and show to friends.

she kept talking anyway. "I know what it is to be taken in the barn and tied up and the blood drawed out of your bare back," she would tell them.

In 1850, Truth attended a meeting in Syracuse, New York. She went to hear white abolitionist George Thompson speak. But she had to force her way onto the stage while the crowd booed.

She said, "I'll tell you what Thompson is going to say to you. He's going to argue that the poor Negroes ought to be out of slavery and in the heavenly state of freedom. But, children, I'm against slavery because I want to keep the white folks who hold slaves from getting sent to hell!" The shocked crowd listened to her quietly.

"When I was a slave away down there in New York, and there was some particularly bad work to be done, some colored woman was sure to be called on to do it."

Sojourner Truth, talking to a man who said that African-Americans were nothing more than apes

FREE LECTURE!

SOJOURNER TRUTH,

Who has been a slave in the State of New York, and who has been a Lecturer for the last twenty-three years, whose characteristics have been so vividly portrayed by Mrs. Harriet Beecher Stowe, as the African Sybil, will deliver a lecture upon the present issues of the day,

At   **On**

And will give her experience as a **Slave mother and religious woman.** She comes highly recommended as a public speaker, having the approval of **many** thousands who have heard her earnest appeals, among whom are **Wendell Phillips, Wm. Lloyd Garrison,** and other distinguished men of the nation.

☞ At the close of her discourse she will offer for sale her photograph and a few of her choice songs.

Pamphlets for Truth's speeches were often passed out on the day of her speech. That didn't keep crowds away. People looked forward to hearing speakers just as many people today look forward to the opening of a new movie. Speeches were a form of entertainment that did not cost much. They also gave people a chance to get out with friends.

The bite of a flea

Speakers at these meetings often spent a lot of time talking about love and peace. Truth believed in these values. But she had learned that the right words did not always mean the right actions. People sometimes forgot to talk about how to stop slavery. So Truth sometimes had to remind people of the problems that needed to be solved.

Sometimes Truth used her sense of humor to win the crowd over to her. Once, at a meeting in Ohio, a man shouted, "Old woman . . . I don't care any more for your talk about slavery than I do for the bite of a flea."

Truth shot back, "Perhaps not, but the Lord willing, I'll keep you scratching."

By this she meant that she would keep on preaching, no matter how much it irritated people.

"Aren't I a woman?"

As she traveled the United States for the freedom of African-Americans, she also noticed how few rights women had. It did not seem fair that men were the only ones with power. They signed the petitions. They gave political support. They had the money. Women seemed on the sidelines of life.

In 1840, William Lloyd Garrison, Lucretia Mott, and Elizabeth Cady Stanton had gone to the World's Anti-slavery Convention in England. The convention organizers would not let the women have seats. Garrison had been shocked. Both he and Stanton had then decided to fight for women's rights as well as freedom for blacks. It was

In 1833, Britain banned slavery in the British Empire. It also halted the shipping of slaves from Africa. This hurt the supply of slaves for the South. It also pressured the U.S. government to outlaw slavery completely. After this, London became a center of abolitionist activities.

obvious that both African-Americans and women were being mistreated.

In 1844 at Northampton, Truth had heard Garrison speak about slavery and women's rights. At the time, she was a gospel preacher who had given her life to preaching about God. But after hearing Garrison, she began to believe that God also wanted her to speak against slavery. In time, she saw that women needed her, too. By 1849, she began working for women's rights.

In 1851, she went to the Woman's Rights Convention in Ohio. After she finished her speech, a man spoke out. He said women were weaker than men, and so they were not equal. Truth was angry.

"That man over there says that women need to be helped into carriages, and lifted over ditches, and to have the best place everywhere," she said. "Nobody ever helps me into carriages, or over mud puddles, or gives me any best place, and aren't I a woman? Look at me! Look at my arm! I have plowed, and planted, and gathered into barns, and no man could head me — and aren't I a woman? I could work as much and eat as much as a man (when I could get it), and bear the lash as well — and aren't I a woman?"

Action, not talk

By now, Sojourner Truth saw that both blacks and women deserved respect. But

Women's fashions of the 1840s and 1850s required a tight corset made of whales' bones. A corset is a tight-fitting piece of clothing that creates a smooth waistline. Women tied the corsets so tightly that they often could not breathe and would then faint. This made people believe that all women were weak.

they were not getting it. White men might appear kind to white women. But Truth knew that kindness could be a trap. A white man could help a woman into a carriage or give her money to buy clothes. But he would not listen to her opinion or give her the right to vote. Her place was in the home, he would say.

So Truth's talks now had three parts: religion, freedom for African-Americans, and women's rights. She soon realized that some people wanted to hear about getting rid of slavery, but did not agree with the idea of women's rights.

She also knew that women had to be bolder. Otherwise, they would not get the rights they wanted. But she also saw that most women did not take action. They did not go to voting places and protest that they could not vote. They did not barge in on their congressmen to convince them. Instead, they sat around and talked about it.

That bothered Truth. At one women's rights convention, she interrupted the talk. "Sisters," she said, "I aren't clear what you be after. If women want any rights more than they got, why don't they just take them and not be talking about it?"

She also felt women were too worried about how they looked. Instead of dressing simply, some women wore the fanciest styles. One time Truth told them

Amelia Jenks Bloomer felt that women couldn't be free until they got rid of the clutter of clothes that they wore. Her pants, called bloomers, took the place of the many petticoats that women wore.

Frances Titus often traveled with Truth. At that time, it was not thought proper for women to travel alone.

Opposite: This photograph shows Truth with papers as if she were reading them. Her followers worried that people might not take her ideas seriously because she could not read.

that they were "dressed in such ridiculous fashion" that their talk about women's rights seemed just as ridiculous. "'Pears to me," she said, "you had better reform yourselves first."

Many women took her words to heart. One woman, Amelia Jenks Bloomer, invented trousers to fit under women's skirts. But, of course, new clothes would not bring equal rights.

Supporting herself

While she traveled, Truth still had to support herself. Often she passed a hat around for money. But that was not enough. In fact, sometimes those funds were stolen right from the hat.

In 1845, former slave Frederick Douglass had published a book about his life. It was called *Narrative of the Life of Frederick Douglass.* It was popular. Olive Gilbert, a friend of Sojourner Truth's, thought Truth should do the same. But Truth felt odd about that because she could not read or write.

Finally Truth told her story to Gilbert, who then wrote it down. The *Narrative of Sojourner Truth* was published in 1850. It covered the events of Truth's life up until her stay at Northampton. Another book, called *The Book of Life,* came out later. It covered her later years.

The first book didn't make much money. So Truth began selling

photographs of herself. "I sell the shadow to support the substance," she wrote on the pictures. To Truth, pictures were only shadows of real people. Between the photographs and the book, she made enough money for her travels.

The nation at war

For years, people in the South disagreed with people in the North. They disagreed about many things, but especially about slavery. The North wanted the South to end slavery. The South needed slaves to work the huge plantations. The North didn't have plantations, so it didn't need as many workers. Yet people in the North gladly accepted the cotton, rice, and other products from the Southern plantations.

In 1861, seven Southern states broke free, or seceded, from the rest of the country. They formed their own government. They also wrote a new constitution and elected Jefferson Davis as their president. They called themselves the Confederate States of America, or the Confederacy.

The remaining states were still called the United States of America, or the Union. They stayed with Abraham Lincoln as president and a government based on the original Constitution. They said the Southern states were wrong to break away.

34

On April 12, 1861, Confederate troops fired on Fort Sumter. This fort was held by Union troops but was located in the Southern city of Charleston, South Carolina. This battle began the Civil War.

Truth and other abolitionists started working for the Union. They believed that if the North lost, hopes for an end to slavery would also be lost. Both Frederick Douglass and Sojourner Truth encouraged African-Americans to join the Union army. Two of Douglass' sons joined. Truth's grandson James Caldwell also joined.

Truth was sorry she was too old to fight. She looked for other ways to help. In 1863, she returned to Battle Creek, Michigan, where she had another house. There she adopted the First Michigan Volunteer Infantry (Colored). It was a troop of black soldiers. She made it her job to keep the soldiers hopeful. She brought them food and often sang for them. She even wrote a song for them to sing. She wanted the black soldiers to have a battle song all their own.

Freeing slaves

The North had a hard time at first. By mid-1862, President Lincoln was afraid that the North would lose if the war went on much longer. So he decided to take action to free the slaves. He hoped this action would end the war. His order,

Slave owners knew that with the Emancipation Proclamation slaves who made it to free territories would never be returned to them. Some owners decided that the best solution was to chase down and kill runaway slaves to frighten other slaves against trying to escape.

called the Emancipation Proclamation, freed all the slaves of the "states . . . in rebellion" on January 1, 1863. It also promised the slaves safety in the North.

Most Northern states had ended slavery earlier, and the proclamation freed slaves only in states that had rebelled. But four states that still allowed slavery in 1863 — Delaware, Kentucky, Maryland, and Missouri — had remained in the Union. Lincoln's proclamation did not apply to them. It also did not free slaves in areas occupied by the Union army. Tennessee, Louisiana, Mississippi, Arkansas, and Virginia had rebelled, but parts of them had been captured by the Union army. The proclamation did not affect slaves in these areas, either.

Thousands of Southern slaves poured into the North. Many whites now had a hard time finding shelter, work, or even clothing. People were afraid. It was one thing to talk of freedom for the slaves. It was another thing to see it happening.

Sojourner Truth saw the mood of her audiences change. Now many who came to hear her speak were angry. Sometimes people yelled "Nigger, nigger!" or refused to let her on stage. Another time, in Indiana, some people tried to make her look like a phony. They thought it would force her to quit speaking. That time, a man said that she seemed more

"Why don't you stir them up? As though an old body like myself could do all the stirring."

Sojourner Truth,
to a newspaper reporter

36

Abolitionists and freed slaves supported the black fighting units. Without them, the black units would not have had uniforms or other supplies. White troops were equipped first.

like a man than a woman. That was not surprising. Truth was about six feet (1.8 meters) tall and very strong.

Sojourner was angry. But she would not be stopped. At once, she proved to them that she was a woman. She pulled back her dress to show them her breast. She knew that it was a wild action to take. But she also knew that it would make them believe her.

"'Sojourner Truth' is the name of a man now lecturing in Kansas City."
St. Louis Dispatch

Black soldiers fight for equality

Many African-Americans joined the Union army. But even as soldiers, they found prejudice. Often they received the worst weapons and the fewest supplies. On top of that, they were paid much less. The black soldiers said this was not fair.

This picture of Sojourner Truth and Abraham Lincoln was actually painted after her death. Diana Corbin, Truth's oldest daughter, posed as Truth. Lincoln's image was copied from another painting.

They said black soldiers often took the most dangerous jobs. So they were doing the most work for the least money.

The black soldiers of the Fifty-fourth and Fifty-fifth Massachusetts Regiments took action. They refused to accept any pay until Congress made it all equal. In 1864, they got what they asked for. Later, in March 1865, they also received equal pay all the way back to the day they had joined the army.

"I felt that I was in the presence of a friend, and I now thank God ... that I always have [supported] his cause, and have done it openly and boldly."
Sojourner Truth, speaking about her visit to Abraham Lincoln

Advice to Lincoln

Truth was sixty-four when the Civil War began. She often wondered when her work would be done. She still devoted her time to both abolition and women's rights. On some days, she spoke in three or four places.

Truth wanted to do more than give speeches in the North. She wanted to make the country's leaders believe that what she said was true. So she decided to travel from Michigan to Washington, D.C. She wanted to talk with President Abraham Lincoln. She had things to tell him. She wanted him to know what African-Americans wanted and needed.

Lincoln welcomed Sojourner Truth. She said later, "I must say, and I am proud to say, that I never was treated by any one with more kindness and cordiality than were shown to me by that great and good man, Abraham Lincoln." Lincoln even autographed her *Book of Life*, writing: "For Aunty Sojourner Truth, October 29, 1864. A. Lincoln."

"With all your opportunities for reading and writing, you don't take hold and do anything. My God, I wonder what you are in the world for!"
Sojourner Truth, to a white audience

Working for the government

By this time, thousands of African-Americans had fled from the South to the North. Many of these former slaves had come to live in Washington, D.C. To help them, government agencies and charity organizations had set up camps called freedmen's villages along Union lines. These camps were nothing more than clusters of shacks. There the people lived in crowded, unhealthy conditions.

And even in the North, blacks had to fear slave traders. Their children were often stolen by whites to work in Northern factories. Truth once heard a government official tell a woman not to make such a fuss about her missing children. Truth remembered Mrs. Dumont saying nearly the same thing to her years earlier after Peter had been sold. "Such a fuss over a little nigger," Mrs. Dumont had said.

Truth decided to stay in Washington, D.C. In late 1864, an organization called the National Freedman's Relief Association asked her to work for them. Her job was to counsel freed slaves living in Arlington Heights, Virginia, near Washington. At last, Truth would be able to help the people.

The Freedmen's Bureau

In March 1865, government officials founded the Freedmen's Bureau. This agency was formed to help the former slaves find jobs and homes. Shortly afterward, the bureau offered Truth a job at the Freedmen's Hospital in Washington, D.C. There, she was to see that black patients received proper care.

Truth had come a long way from her days as a little slave girl. She was now almost seventy years old. But she felt she still had much to do. She spent much of her time teaching freed slaves how to take control of their lives. She knew this was not an easy thing to learn. But she

"With no education from books or contact with the world aside from plantation life — hungry, thirsty, ragged, homeless — they were the [image] of Despair."
An observer writing on the plight of the freed slaves

"These places can be considered as nothing better than [breeding] grounds of crime, disease, and death."
A. C. Richards, superintendent of police, Washington, D.C., surveying the freedmen's villages

This drawing makes the freedmen's village look large and roomy. In reality, the village homes were closely packed shacks.

had done it. As she told her grandson and traveling companion, Sam Banks, "They have to learn to be free."

The war ends; Lincoln is shot

Truth was still in Washington, D.C., when the Civil War ended. On April 9, 1865, Confederate general Robert E. Lee surrendered to Union general Ulysses S. Grant in Virginia. But before the Union could rejoice, President Lincoln was killed. John Wilkes Booth shot the president at Ford's Theatre on April 14, 1865. The country was shocked.

Vice President Andrew Johnson became president. He did not share Lincoln's ideas on equality. He was a Southerner and wanted to focus on rebuilding the South. Truth was worried that human rights would be ignored.

"Sojourner Truth has good ideas about the industry and virtue of the colored people. I commend her energetic and faithful efforts . . . in promoting order, cleanliness, industry, and virtue."

John Eaton, Jr., on appointing Sojourner to the Freedmen's Bureau

41

JIM CROW LAW.

HELD BY THE UNITED STATES SUPREME COURT.

Inte Within the Competency of the Louisiana Legislature and Railroads—Must Furnish Separate Cars for Whites and Blacks.

Many legislators tried to get rid of Jim Crow laws. They argued against having "separate but equal" societies for black people and white people. To many, it made as much sense as having separate facilities for short people and tall people.

Prejudice continues

In December 1865, the Thirteenth Amendment to the Constitution became law. This law ended slavery in the United States. Truth was overjoyed. After all her years of preaching against it, slavery was finally finished.

But Truth was not finished. She wanted to see African-Americans vote, run for office, and own property. That was not going to be an easy task in the South. Many Southerners would not obey the laws of the federal government. For years, the Southern states had been passing laws called the Black Codes. These laws were used to control Southern blacks.

Secret groups of white citizens made sure that African-Americans obeyed these laws. These groups used violence against those who fought for their rights. They burned many black people's homes, kidnapped their children, and often even killed people. One of these secret groups, the Ku Klux Klan, began in 1865 and still exists today.

Jim Crow laws

The Black Codes had long controlled many areas of black life. After the Civil War ended, "Jim Crow" laws appeared. The Jim Crow laws supposedly created a "separate but equal" black society. They called for blacks and whites to be separated, or segregated. Each group had separate businesses, restaurants, schools, and even streetcars. But what this often meant was that the African-Americans got the worst in everything.

These laws were felt even in Washington, D.C. The city street railroad had one car called the Jim Crow car for black passengers. Sojourner Truth would not accept this. She had worked hard for her freedom and human rights. She was going to sit wherever she wanted.

She complained to the president of the street railroad. He removed the Jim Crow car. But many white conductors did not want African-Americans sitting with whites. Many of these drivers would not stop for black passengers.

Truth would run after the cars and demand a seat. One time, a conductor

"There is a great stir about colored men getting their rights, but not a word about the colored women; and if colored men get their rights, and not colored women theirs, you see the colored men will be masters over the women, and it will be just as bad as it was before."
Sojourner Truth

Equal rights didn't guarantee respect for African-Americans. Black people in cartoons were often made to look silly. This may have seemed funny to some. But it also encouraged the idea of African-Americans as an inferior class.

hurt her arm when he tried to push her off the car. Truth sued him in court. Again, she won. She might not be able to change what people believed. But she could make them obey the laws.

Whose rights?

The Thirteenth Amendment freed the slaves. But it did not make them U.S. citizens. But then, the Constitution did not let women enjoy the full rights of American citizens either.

Truth said that women should have the same rights as men. At one rally, she said that giving these rights to black men but not black women would just create a new kind of slavery. Women would have men as their new masters.

After Lincoln died, Congress passed the Fourteenth Amendment. The states approved it in 1868. This amendment made it illegal to pass laws against blacks. (But in many states, Jim Crow laws lasted for years.) It said that people born or naturalized in the United States were citizens and gave male citizens the right to vote. But because many blacks had been born in Africa, they still were not citizens and could not vote.

"We want as much!"

In 1870, black men were finally allowed to vote. The Fifteenth Amendment guaranteed the right to vote for all men,

no matter what race. But it did not say anything about women.

Truth was seventy-three years old now. She had leg ulcers, and an infection had nearly killed her. But she knew she had one more fight ahead. She had to stay strong and loud to fight for the rights of women.

She believed that all women were treated unfairly. But she felt black women had the worst situation. White women received certain rights because of their husbands. They usually had more money and power. But because slaves had been sold so often, black women often had no husbands. So, unlike white women, black women often had to support themselves and their children.

Truth fought hard for women's rights. "I have done a great deal of work," she would say. "As much as a man, but did

The Fourteenth and Fifteenth Amendments were major victories against slavery. This print celebrates some of those victories. But African-Americans still had a long way to go. Many whites still saw black people as inferior or thought they could do only the simplest jobs.

"Well, children, where there is so much racket there must be something out of kilter. I think that 'twixt the niggers of the South and the women at the North all talking about rights, the white men will be in a fix pretty soon."
Sojourner Truth

not get so much pay. I used to work in the field and bind grain . . . but men doing no more, got twice as much pay. . . . We do as much, we eat as much, we want as much."

Many people said that women were not equal to men. They said women were weaker by nature and were not smart enough to vote. For these reasons, they claimed that women should not have as many rights.

Sojourner Truth knew these were all excuses. It came down to white men not wanting to give up their control. She told one group of men, "You have been having our rights so long that you think, like a slave-holder, that you own us. I know that it is hard for one who had held the reins for so long to give it up; it cuts like a knife. It will feel all the better when it closes up again."

> "Did Jesus ever say anything against women? Not a word. But he did speak awful hard things against the men. You know what they were. And he knew them to be true. But he didn't say nothing against the women."
>
> Sojourner Truth

> "Now I hear talking about the Constitution and the rights of man. I come up and I take hold of this Constitution. It looks mighty big, and I feel for my rights, but there aren't any there. Then I says, God, what ails this Constitution? He says to me, 'Sojourner, there is a little weevil in it.'"
>
> Sojourner Truth

Breaking the chain

Women all over the country tried to convince Congress to give them the right to vote. The lawmakers would not listen.

Many women decided they had had enough talk. It was time for action. Following Sojourner Truth, women began going to voting places to register to vote. They failed many times but would not give up.

Women had focused their efforts on the right to vote. They knew that when they could vote they could elect men and women who would help them. They could then push for laws giving women equal pay. They could rewrite the laws to make women equal to men in every way.

Truth believed it was her job to win equal rights for all people. And she believed God was urging her in her work. She said, "I suppose I am kept here because something remains for me to do. I suppose I am yet to help break the chain." This "chain" kept people from enjoying their human rights.

Trapped in the slums

Truth was still concerned about the Southern blacks now living in Northern cities. Before they were freed, most of them had worked in the fields. That was the life and work that they knew. But now they were jammed into the city slums. They were not used to city life. They did not have skills for the jobs there. The slaves had done all the work for the white man. So now Truth felt that the government owed them something. An idea came to her.

In 1870, she went to talk with President Ulysses S. Grant. She told him that thousands of acres of land in the West had been given to the railroads to help trains go west. Truth felt there was more than enough land there for that. She asked Grant to give some of the western lands to the freed slaves. He listened, but did not agree with her.

So in April of that year, she went to Congress. One congressman told her that she must bring a petition from the people. A petition is a written request for a change, signed by several people. She asked him to help her write one. He did.

More hatred

She began carrying the petition with her in her travels. She gathered signatures wherever she went. She even made a special trip to Kansas to talk to the settlers about her plan.

On this trip, Truth learned that some white people did not like her idea. They were afraid that her plan would give blacks control of the western territories. Some newspaper reporters wrote terrible things about Truth. One from New Jersey wrote: "We do most decidedly dislike the complexion and everything else [about] Mrs. Truth. . . . She is a crazy, ignorant, repelling negress." This hurt Truth. But it also made her want to work even harder for her dream, no matter what people said.

Not all newspapers were against her. An editor from a Rochester, New York, paper wrote, "Her subject is the condition of the freed colored people dependent on the government. . . . Let Rochester give her a cordial reception."

Harriet Beecher Stowe, author of Uncle Tom's Cabin. *Stowe's book made people look seriously at slavery. It changed many people's views. Some people believe it was one of the causes of the Civil War. Abraham Lincoln once called Stowe the "little lady who wrote the book that made this great war."*

Her message was simple. "Let the freedmen be emptied out in the West," she said. "Give them land. . . . teach them to read, and then they will be somebody." She believed that if that happened, the African-Americans would no longer be "trash" in the streets.

"Her whole air had at times a gloomy sort of [humor] which impressed one strangely."
    Harriet Beecher Stowe, on meeting Sojourner Truth

Tragedy and more sickness

But Sojourner Truth was growing old. She found it hard to keep up the pace she had been keeping for years. By 1880, she was exhausted. For ten long years she had traveled, speaking on the rights of women and blacks. She had been to twenty-one states and Washington, D.C.

She had walked much of the way. Her leg ulcers often pained her. Then in 1875, her grandson Sam Banks died. Sam was Elizabeth's son. He was also Truth's favorite grandson and her companion. He had been traveling with her since he was five years old. His death made her very sad. After it, she grew even weaker.

Even though she was sick, Truth managed to travel to Philadelphia in 1876 to celebrate the United States' one-hundredth birthday. As usual, she lectured on giving land to former slaves and on women's right to vote. It was one of her last trips.

"Won't that be glorious!"

Until she died, Truth had been returning often to her home in Battle Creek, Michigan. When she came home, her doctor, John Kellogg, tried to take good care of her. But she was a stubborn patient. As soon as she felt well, she would begin traveling again. That made her weak all over again.

By 1883, her leg ulcers were very serious. Kellogg could not heal them. Truth tried to fix them herself using a medicine made for horses. That only made the infection worse and caused terrible fevers. Even from her bed, Truth continued working. As friends gathered at her side, she had them write letters about her causes.

"The Lord has put new flesh on to old bones."
Sojourner Truth, when her leg ulcer healed for a time

"Well, doctor, I thought those . . . medicines you gave me were too mild for anyone as tough as I am, so I went to the horse doctor and he gave me something that was real strong!"
Sojourner Truth

Sojourner Truth was buried in Battle Creek, Michigan. Later, the people there had a memorial built for her. They also have a big celebration every year to honor Truth's contributions to the struggle for blacks' and women's rights.

Truth never lost her faith. She compared death to stepping out into the light. "Oh, won't that be glorious!" she once said. And just before she died, she told her friends and children, "I'm not going to die, honey; I'm going home like a shooting star."

Truth died on November 26, 1883. She was eighty-six years old.

Respect

By the time of her death, Truth had gained the respect she sought. Even people who disagreed with her views admired her strong will. People across the country saw how tirelessly she had worked for her beliefs. One Battle Creek newspaper editor wrote, "This country has lost one of its most remarkable personages." Former slave Frederick Douglass called her independent and courageous. Many people agreed; more than one thousand attended her funeral.

In Battle Creek, people worked to keep Truth's memory alive. They marked her grave with a granite tombstone and built a museum to celebrate her life and work. They also encouraged the Detroit Historical Museum to include a painting of Truth in its collection.

But still, many people have never heard of Sojourner Truth. Although she worked for many different causes, she is not as famous as people like Frederick Douglass and Susan B. Anthony. Even so, her memory lives on. Her life laid the groundwork for the future of both women and African-Americans. Her lessons have been followed. Her words are remembered.

Her work continues

Over one hundred years after her death, Truth's work is still being carried out by other people. Some of her causes have ended in victory. For example, the Nineteenth Amendment gave women the right to vote in 1920.

Another amendment passed in 1964 would have made Truth happy. The Twenty-fourth Amendment, called the Poll Tax Amendment, made it illegal to charge people money to vote. To keep

Opposite: Martin Luther King, Jr., encouraged African-Americans to fight for equal rights through peaceful protest. He was guided in his work by the Bible, the teachings of Mahatma Gandhi, and his readings on the antislavery movement.

people from voting, Southern states had been charging people a tax to vote. Poorer people — usually black people — often could not pay. So they could not vote. The Poll Tax Amendment made those taxes illegal.

Over the next several years, many more laws were passed to protect the rights of minorities. In 1964 and 1968, two Civil Rights Acts were passed. They made it illegal to treat someone differently because of color, race, religion, or sex. These rules applied mainly to jobs. But they also made it clear that unfair treatment would no longer be allowed in public places such as hotels, restaurants, and theaters.

One hundred years after Truth had spoken out so strongly for equality, something happened that would have made her angry. In 1972, Congress passed the Equal Rights Amendment. It would have made sure that all citizens had equal rights whether they were female or male. Women would finally have rights equal to those of men. But this amendment had to be passed by many states and some did not approve it. So the amendment did not become law.

Organized power

Many groups today owe their power to the early abolitionists like Sojourner Truth and to the women's rights

W.E.B. DuBOIS CLUB
HOUGH PROJECT

JOBS
PEACE
FREEDOM

JOBS
PEACE
FREEDOM

"Fellow Negroes, is it not time to be men? Is it not time to strike back when we are struck? Is it not high time to hold up our heads and clench our teeth and swear by the Eternal God we will not be slaves and that no aider, abettor, and teacher of slavery in any shape or guise can longer lead us?"
W.E.B. DuBois, The Crises, 1913 (from Freedomways, 1st quarter, 1965.)

JOIN
NOW

FREEDOM
NOW

1844 E. 81ST   •   PHONE: 791-5179

W. E. B. Du Bois earned a degree from Harvard University and taught at Atlanta University. But with all his education, he could not even drink from the same water fountain as whites or sit in the same section of the courthouse. He helped form the National Association for the Advancement of Colored People (NAACP). This organization gave African-Americans the strength to fight unfair laws and customs. It still does today.

movement of the 1800s. One of these groups is called the National Association for the Advancement of Colored People (NAACP). Formed in 1909, its purpose was to get rid of "all barriers to . . . equality" for African-Americans.

In many places in recent years, blacks were still being treated unfairly. Jim Crow laws and local customs still kept them from using the restaurants, hotels, drinking fountains, and bathrooms that whites used. And they often got the worst houses, schools, and jobs.

The NAACP went to court to fight against unfair laws. Other organizations, such as the National Urban League and the Southern Christian Leadership Conference (SCLC), used different methods. These organizations used

Over one hundred years after the first women's rights convention, women continue to fight for their issues.
In this photograph, women salute the Equal Rights Amendment at the 1977 national convention of the National Organization for Women (NOW).

methods such as demonstrations and strikes to fight for changes.

Women saw positive changes come about for African-Americans. So they began to get organized, too. The National Organization for Women (NOW) formed in 1966 to push for equality for women. One of NOW's main issues is equal pay for equal work. Truth worked hard for this cause in her travels. NOW members can thank Sojourner Truth for pointing the way.

Truth's influence

Two modern leaders shared many of Sojourner Truth's values. These leaders were Martin Luther King, Jr., and Mahatma Gandhi. Both believed in equality, freedom, and nonviolence.

Gandhi was from India, which was held by the British. When he was a young law student in England, he read many of the abolitionist writings. Later, he used ideas from his readings to lead his country to independence from Britain. Like Sojourner Truth before him, he was especially drawn to equality for all and nonviolence.

But he took it a step further. Truth had believed in nonviolence for herself, an individual. Gandhi saw nonviolence as a way to promote change. He introduced nonviolent protest to his followers. He saw it as a way for the Indians to demand freedom from their British rulers.

Truth had said that no one could be free as long as some people were treated as second-class citizens. Gandhi agreed

"I have a dream that one day this nation will rise up and live out the true meaning of its creed: 'We hold these truths to be self-evident: that all men are created equal.' I have a dream that one day on the red hills of Georgia the sons of former slaves and the sons of former slave owners will be able to sit down together at the table of brotherhood. . . . I have a dream that my four little children will one day live in a nation where they will be judged not by the color of their skin, but by the content of their character."

Martin Luther King, Jr., in his famous 1963 speech

57

with these thoughts. He fought — peacefully — for equal rights for all.

Martin Luther King, Jr., respected Gandhi's ideals. He led the black civil rights movement in the United States during the 1950s and 1960s. The purpose of this movement was to make the government fully protect the rights of African-Americans. Blacks had been promised this nearly one hundred years earlier. King used peaceful protest to force the government to keep its promise.

"I have done the best I could"

Sojourner Truth left her mark. It can be seen in the way her words and beliefs continue to bring change as people learn about her life. She liked to fight for what she believed. So do her followers.

Young Belle left Dumont's farm in 1826 to later become Sojourner Truth. She knew that her journey would not be easy. But she also knew that it would be a glorious journey that would bring change. In every crisis of her life, Truth took action and demanded justice.

Sojourner Truth knew that she might not live to see all of her work finished. But she also knew that the things she had fought for were right. So she believed that her work would one day be done. "I have done the best I could," she told her friends as she was dying. "I have told the whole truth."

To find out more . . .

Organizations

The groups listed below can give you more information about Sojourner Truth and about the civil and women's rights movements. When you write to them, tell them exactly what you would like to know, and include your name, address, and age.

Communiqu'Elles
3585 St.-Urbain
Montreal, Quebec
Canada H2X 2N6

Detroit Public Library
5201 Woodward Avenue
Detroit, MI 48202

Kimball House Museum
196 Capital Avenue NE
Battle Creek, MI 49017

National Organization for
   Women (NOW)
1000 16th Street NW, Suite 700
Washington, DC 20036

National Action Committee on
   the Status of Women
344 Bloor Street West, Suite 505
Toronto, Ontario
Canada M5S 3A7

National Association for the
   Advancement of Colored
   People (NAACP)
4805 Mount Hope Drive
Baltimore, MD 21215

Ontario Black History Society
Ontario Heritage Center
10 Adelaide Street East, Suite 202
Toronto, Ontario
Canada M5C 1J3

Books

The following books will help you learn more about Sojourner Truth and slavery and about the civil rights and women's rights movements. Check your local library or bookstore to see if they have them or can order them for you.

About Sojourner Truth —

Journey Toward Freedom: The Story of Sojourner Truth. Jacqueline Bernard (Grosset & Dunlap)

Sojourner Truth and the Struggle for Freedom. Edward B. Claflin
(Barron's Educational Series)
Sojourner Truth: Slave, Abolitionist, Fighter for Women's Rights.
Aletha Jane Lindstrom (Julian Messner)
Walking the Road to Freedom: A Story about Sojourner Truth. Jeri
Ferris (Carolrhoda Books)

About slavery and freedom —

Frederick Douglass: Freedom Fighter. Lillie Patterson (Garrard)
*Harriet and the Runaway Book: The Story of Harriet Beecher Stowe
and* Uncle Tom's Cabin. Johanna Johnston (Harper & Row
Junior Books)
Harriet Tubman: Guide to Freedom. Sam Epstein and Beryl
Epstein (Garrard)

About civil and women's rights —

The Civil Rights Movement in America from 1865 to the Present.
Frederick McKissock and Patricia McKissock (Childrens Press)
Elizabeth Cady Stanton. Jan Gleiter and Kathleen Thompson
(Raintree)
Every Kid's Guide to Understanding Human Rights. Joy Berry
(Childrens Press)
Jesse Jackson: A Black Leader. Patricia S. Martin (Rourke Corp.)
Mahatma Gandhi. Beverley Birch (Gareth Stevens)
The Story of Susan B. Anthony. Susan Clinton (Childrens Press)

List of new words

abolitionism
A movement against slavery. Abolitionism began in Britain and
France during the late eighteenth century and quickly spread to
the United States. It gained many followers there during the
American Revolution. Before the Civil War, many abolitionists
helped many Southern slaves escape to the Northern free states
or to Canada. They often used a system of escape routes and

safe houses known as the Underground Railroad. The term
abolitionism comes from the word *abolish*, which means "to get
rid of" or "to end." (See also **Underground Railroad**.)

African-Americans

A term used to refer to people known in North America as
blacks. Over the centuries, language referring to the people now
known as blacks or African-Americans has changed. Slaves
brought to the Americas in the seventeenth and eighteenth
centuries were simply called *Africans* by slave traders and
owners. During the eighteenth century, the term *Negro* came
into use, from the Spanish and Portuguese word *negro*, meaning
"black." Later, the civil rights movement of the 1960s brought
back the term *black* again. Today people use both *African-
American* and *black*.

amendment

A change or improvement. Amendments to the U.S.
Constitution must be proposed, or suggested, by Congress and
accepted by three-fourths of the states to become law.

Constitution of the United States

The document that sets forth the basic structure, principles, and
limits of the United States government.

discrimination

Treating a person or persons differently based on race, sex,
religion, or other characteristics.

Douglass, Frederick (1817-1895)

An escaped slave who became a leader in the fight against
slavery. Douglass was a powerful speaker. He used his talent to
speak out against slavery all across the country. Douglass later
began a newspaper for blacks in Rochester, New York.

Fourteenth Amendment

The amendment to the U.S. Constitution that defines all persons

born or naturalized in the United States as citizens. It also
says that states may not deprive anyone of life, liberty, or
property without fair procedures, such as a trial. This
amendment was approved in 1868.

freedmen's villages
Camps set up by the federal government near the end of the
Civil War. These camps housed thousands of slaves who were
escaping north to freedom. The government provided the
former slaves with housing, food, and medical care.

Fugitive Slave Laws
Two federal laws passed to help slave owners recapture
runaway slaves. One was passed in 1793. The other became
law in 1850. These laws were often ignored. Many people in the
North were against slavery and would not help slave owners
recapture runaway slaves. This made Southern slave owners
angry. The law of 1850 forced federal marshals to help slave
owners catch runaways. Marshals could be fined if slaves
escaped from their custody. This law also denied slaves' rights.

Garrison, William Lloyd (1805-1879)
A powerful leader of the abolitionist movement, as well as
founder and editor of an antislavery newspaper, the *Liberator*.
Garrison was also a strong supporter of women's rights.

integration
The process of uniting different groups, such as races, into one
society or organization.

Phillips, Wendell (1811-1884)
An abolitionist leader and political reformer. He was a follower
of William Lloyd Garrison and led the struggle for the
Fourteenth and Fifteenth Amendments to the U.S. Constitution.

Quakers
A common name for members of the religious group called the

Society of Friends. The basic teaching of this group is that there is something of God in everyone. Quakers work to create a peaceful society free of human evil. Early Quakers fought for many causes and worked especially hard against slavery.

ratify
To officially approve. Thirty-eight states are now needed to ratify an amendment to the U.S. Constitution.

segregation
The practice of forming separate societies or organizations based on race, class, or other group differences. In the United States, segregation by race was practiced even after slavery was ended. This kept blacks and whites apart in employment, schooling, housing, and many other areas. Segregation by race still exists today even though it is against the law. Blacks and other minorities are often isolated in slums. And they are often overlooked for good jobs.

sovereignty
Independence and control, especially of and for a political body. The Southern states wanted control, or sovereignty, over issues, such as slavery, that they thought affected only their states.

Stanton, Elizabeth Cady (1815-1902)
A founder of the women's rights movement in the United States. Stanton was a strong leader in the fight to win voting and property rights for women.

Stowe, Harriet Beecher (1811-1896)
An abolitionist and writer. In her book *Uncle Tom's Cabin*, Stowe showed how awful slavery was. This powerful book encouraged the antislavery movement in the United States. Stowe also wrote poetry, short stories, antislavery articles, and other novels.

Underground Railroad
A secret system that helped slaves escape to free states or to

Canada. It was organized and run by Northern blacks and abolitionists. The system included secret routes and various stopping points, called safe houses, that provided clothing, shelter, and food to the slaves.

Important dates

1797 Isabella, or Belle, is born to slaves Baumfree and Mau-Mau Bett Hardenbergh on the Hardenbergh farm in Ulster County, New York.

1799 The first New York Emancipation Act is passed, stating that slaves born after July 4, 1799, would be freed when they reached a certain age. Females were to be freed at age twenty-five. Males were to be freed at age twenty-eight.

1806 Nine-year-old Belle is sold to John Neely.

1807 Mau-Mau Bett dies.

1808 John Neely sells Belle to Martin Schryver.

1810 Martin Schryver sells Belle to John Dumont.

1814 At seventeen, Belle is forced to marry Thomas.

1815 Diana, Belle's first child, is born. Over the next ten years, Belle gives birth to Peter, Elizabeth, Sophia, and possibly a fourth daughter who dies in infancy.

1818 The New York state legislature passes a law freeing all slaves, no matter what their age, as of July 4, 1827.

1826 Belle claims her freedom and leaves John Dumont's farm.

1827 Belle's son, Peter, is traded to a farmer in Alabama. Belle sues his owner and wins him back.

1829	Belle moves to New York City. She begins working for Elijah Pierson.
1833	Belle moves to Sing Sing, New York, to be part of the Kingdom, a utopian religious community. The American Anti-Slavery Society is formed.
1843	At forty-six, Belle decides to become a traveling preacher. She takes the name Sojourner Truth.
1850	In Worcester, Massachusetts, Sojourner attends her first women's rights convention. The Fugitive Slave Law is passed. The *Narrative of Sojourner Truth* is published.
1861	**February** — Seven Southern states secede from the Union and form the Confederate States of America. In April, four more Southern states secede. **March 4** — Abraham Lincoln becomes president. **April 12** — The Civil War begins.
1863	**January 1** — Union president Lincoln's Emancipation Proclamation frees slaves in all Confederate areas.
1864	**October 29** — Truth meets with Lincoln. She is commissioned as a counselor for the freedmen's village in Arlington, Virginia.
1865	The Freedmen's Bureau is established. Truth is appointed to the Freedmen's Hospital in Washington, D.C. **April 9** — Confederate general Robert E. Lee surrenders to Union general Ulysses S. Grant. **April 14** — John Wilkes Booth shoots and kills Lincoln. **December** — The Thirteenth Amendment, which abolishes slavery in all the states, is ratified.

1868 The Fourteenth Amendment is ratified. It grants citizenship to all people born or naturalized in the United States but protects only adult males' right to vote.

1870 **March 30** — The Fifteenth Amendment is ratified. It grants black men the right to vote.
March 31 — Sojourner meets President Ulysses S. Grant. Truth begins touring again, speaking for women's rights and calling for land in the West to be given to free blacks.

1875 Sam Banks, Truth's grandson and companion, dies.

1876 Truth recovers from an extended illness and attends the Centennial Exposition in Philadelphia.

1883 **November 26** — Sojourner Truth dies at home in Battle Creek, Michigan.

1909 The National Association for the Advancement of Colored People (NAACP) is founded.

1964 The Civil Rights Act of 1964 becomes law. This act prohibits discrimination in employment and in public places, such as restaurants, hotels, and theaters.

1966 The National Organization for Women (NOW) is established to promote the rights of women.

1968 Congress passes the Civil Rights Act of 1968, prohibiting discrimination in housing and real estate sales.

1972 The Equal Rights Amendment (ERA) passes Congress. It states that neither the states nor the federal government may deny or restrict equal rights on account of sex. The required number of states fails to ratify and the proposed amendment expires in 1982.

Index

J   Tolan, Mary M.
B
Truth   Sojourner Truth.